THE PETER YARROW SONGBOOK

Sleepytime Songs

ILLUSTRATED BY

Terry Widener

STERLING

New York / London

I dedicate this book to Pete Seeger, Josh White, the Weavers, Burl Ives, Woody Guthrie—and to Vera Yarrow,
who introduced her son to them all, and inspired him by blazing the trail long before he knew he would be following it.

I dedicate my performances on the accompanying CD to my delightful and sparkling granddaughter,
Valentina, and to my two children with shining souls, Bethany and Christopher, with lasting memories
of the bedtime stories and songs we shared that paved the way for us to become the dearest of lifelong friends.

❧

STERLING and the distinctive Sterling logo are registered trademarks of Sterling Publishing Co., Inc.

Library of Congress Cataloging-in-Publication Data
Peter Yarrow songbook : sleepytime songs / [compiled by] Peter Yarrow ; illustrated by Terry Widener.
p. cm.
ISBN 978-1-4027-5962-8
1. Lullabies, English--United States--Texts. 2. Folk songs, English--United States--Texts. I. Yarrow, Peter, 1938- II. Widener, Terry, ill.
M1628.P48 2008   782.42162'1300268--dc22   2008022530

2 4 6 8 10 9 7 5 3 1

Published by Sterling Publishing Co., Inc. 387 Park Avenue South, New York, NY 10016
All songs are traditional with new lyrics and music by Peter Yarrow and Bethany Yarrow © 2008 Silver Dawn Music, ASCAP
with the exception of "Puff the Magic Dragon." "Puff, The Magic Dragon" © Silver Dawn Music. "Puff, The Magic Dragon"
(Peter Yarrow/Lenny Lipton) © 1963 Pepamar Music, ASCAP, Renewed 1991, Silver Dawn Music, administered by WB Music Corp.
(ASCAP)/Honalee Melodies administered by Cherry Lane Music Publishing Co. Inc. (ASCAP)

New lyrics and music by Peter Yarrow and Bethany Yarrow © 2008 Silver Dawn Music
Additional text © 2008 by Peter Yarrow
Illustrations © 2008 by Terry Widener

The artwork for this book was created using acrylic paints.
Designed by Scott Piehl

Distributed in Canada by Sterling Publishing c/o Canadian Manda Group, 165 Dufferin Street Toronto, Ontario, Canada M6K 3H6
Distributed in the United Kingdom by GMC Distribution Services Castle Place, 166 High Street, Lewes, East Sussex, England BN7 1XU
Distributed in Australia by Capricorn Link (Australia) Pty. Ltd.P.O. Box 704, Windsor, NSW 2756, Australia

Printed in China
All rights reserved

Sterling ISBN 978-1-4027-5962-8

For information about custom editions, special sales, premium and corporate purchases, please contact
Sterling Special Sales Department at 800-805-5489 or specialsales@sterlingpublishing.com.

CONTENTS

PETER YARROW

Each of the songs in this collection contains a message to your children that they will come to understand more and more deeply as the years pass by. Through these songs you can tell your children that you not only love them, but that you love them as much as you've ever loved anybody or anything in your life. In the sound of your voice they will hear your hopes, your dreams, and sense the depth of your love for them. They will come to know that, to you, their happiness comes first, and knowing that will strengthen them and sustain them in the years to come. They will never forget that you have cared enough to put the ordinary concerns of life aside to spend this special time with them.

Sing to them at bedtime, at naptime, in quiet times. Whisper or say the lyrics, or sing them along with my daughter, Bethany, and me. To your children, your voice, spoken, sung, or whispered, will be the most comforting and beautiful music of all, and provide precious memories that will last well into their adulthoods.

All Through the Night

Sleep, my child, and peace attend thee
All through the night.
Guardian angels God will send thee
All through the night.

Soft the drowsy hours are creeping,
Hill and dale in slumber steeping.
I, my loved one, watch am keeping
All through the night.

Puff, the Magic Dragon

Puff, the magic dragon, lived by the sea,
And frolicked in the autumn mist
    in a land called Honalee.
Little Jackie Paper loved that rascal Puff,
And brought him strings and sealing wax
    and other fancy stuff.

Puff, the magic dragon, lived by the sea,
And frolicked in the autumn mist in a land called Honalee.
Puff, the magic dragon, lived by the sea,
And frolicked in the autumn mist in a land called Honalee.

Together they would travel on a boat with billowed sail.
Jackie kept a lookout perched on Puff's gigantic tail.
Noble kings and princes would bow whene'er they came.
Pirate ships would lower their flag when
    Puff roared out his name.

Puff, the magic dragon, lived by the sea,
And frolicked in the autumn mist in a land called Honalee.
Puff, the magic dragon, lived by the sea,
And frolicked in the autumn mist in a land called Honalee.

A dragon lives forever, but not so little girls and boys.
Painted wings and giants' rings make way for other toys.
One gray night it happened, Jackie Paper came no more,
So Puff, that mighty dragon, he ceased his fearless roar.

His head was bent in sorrow, and green scales
    fell like rain.
Puff no longer went to play along the cherry lane.
Without his lifelong friend, Puff could not be brave,
So Puff, that mighty dragon, sadly slipped into his cave.

Puff, the magic dragon, lives by the sea,
And frolicks in the autumn mist in a land called Honalee.
Puff, the magic dragon, still lives by the sea,
And frolicks in the autumn mist in a land called Honalee.

Ole Blue

I had a dog and his name was Blue,
I had a dog and his name was Blue,
I had a dog and his name was Blue,
I betcha five dollars he's a good dog too.

Cryin', "Here, Blue! You good dog, you."

Ole Blue come when I blow my horn,
Ole Blue come when I blow my horn.
Blue come a-runnin' through the yellow corn.
Ole Blue come when I blow my horn.

Cryin', "Here, Blue! You good dog, you."

Blue chased a possum up a hollow limb,
Blue chased a possum up a hollow limb,
Blue chased a possum up a hollow limb,
Ole Blue growled, possum grinned at him.

Cryin', "Here, Blue! You good dog, you."

When Ole Blue died, he died so hard,
Ole Blue died, he died so hard,
Ole Blue died, he died so hard,
He shook the ground in my backyard.

Cryin', "Here, Blue! You good dog, you."

One more thing you got to know,
One more thing before you go,
One more thing you got to know,
Blue's gone to heaven where the good dogs go.

Cryin', "Here, Blue! You good dog, you."

I had a dog and his name was Blue,
I had a dog and his name was Blue,
I had a dog and his name was Blue,
I betcha five dollars he's a good dog too.

Cryin', "Here, Blue! You good dog, you."
Cryin', "Here, Blue! You good dog, you."

All the Pretty Little Horses

Hush-a-bye, don't you cry,
Go to sleepy, little baby.
When you wake, you shall have
All the pretty little horses.

Dapples and grays, pintos and bays,
All the pretty little horses.

Way down yonder, in the meadow,
Poor little baby crying, "Mama."
Bees and the butterflies flutter round its eyes,
Poor little baby crying, "Mama."

Hush-a-bye, don't you cry,
Go to sleepy, little baby.
When you wake, you shall have
All the pretty little horses.

Hush, Little Baby

Hush, little baby, don't say a word,
Mama's gonna buy you a mockingbird.

And if that mockingbird don't sing,
Papa's gonna buy you a diamond ring.

And if that diamond ring turns brass,
Mama's gonna buy you a looking glass.

And if that looking glass gets broke,
Papa's gonna buy you a billy goat.

And if that billy goat don't pull,
Mama's gonna buy you a cart and bull.

And if that cart and bull turns over,
Papa's gonna buy you a doggie named Rover.

And if that doggie named Rover don't bark,
Mama's gonna buy you a horse and cart.

And if that horse and cart falls down,
You'll still be the sweetest little baby in town.

Kumbaya

Kumbaya, my Lord, kumbaya,
Kumbaya, my Lord, kumbaya,
Kumbaya, my Lord, kumbaya,
Oh, Lord, kumbaya.

Someone's singing, Lord, kumbaya,
Someone's singing, Lord, kumbaya,
Someone's singing, Lord, kumbaya,
Oh, Lord, kumbaya.

Someone's laughing, Lord, kumbaya,
Someone's laughing, Lord, kumbaya,
Someone's laughing, Lord, kumbaya,
Oh, Lord, kumbaya.

Someone's crying, Lord, kumbaya,
Someone's crying, Lord, kumbaya,
Someone's crying, Lord, kumbaya,
Oh, Lord, kumbaya.

Someone's praying, Lord, kumbaya,
Someone's praying, Lord, kumbaya,
Someone's praying, Lord, kumbaya,
Oh, Lord, kumbaya.

Someone's sleeping, Lord, kumbaya,
Someone's sleeping, Lord, kumbaya,
Someone's sleeping, Lord, kumbaya,
Oh, Lord, kumbaya.

The Water Is Wide

The water is wide, I cannot get o'er,
Neither have I the wings to fly.
Build me a boat that can carry two,
And both shall row, my love and I.

I leaned my back against an oak,
Thinking it was a trusty tree.
But first it bent and then it broke,
Just as my love proved false to me.

Oh, love is handsome and love is fine,
Gay as a jewel when first it's new.
But love grows old and it waxeth cold,
And fades away like morning dew.

The water is wide, I cannot get o'er,
Neither have I the wings to fly.
Build me a boat that can carry two,
And both shall row, my love and I.

Down in the Valley

Down in the valley, the valley so low,
Hang your head over, hear the wind blow.
Hear the wind blow, love, hear the wind blow,
Hang your head over, hear the wind blow.

Roses love sunshine, violets love dew,
Angels in heaven knows I love you.
Knows I love you, dear, knows I love you,
Angels in heaven knows I love you.

I knew I loved you, right from the start.
Say that you love me, and we'll never part.
We'll never part, love, we'll never part.
Say that you love me, we'll never part.

Down in the valley, the valley so low,
Hang your head over, hear the wind blow.
Hear the wind blow, love, hear the wind blow,
Hang your head over, hear the wind blow.

All My Trials

Hush, little baby, don't you cry,
You know your mama someday will fly.
All my trials, Lord, soon be over.

I had a little book was given to me,
And every page spelled liberty.
All my trials, Lord, soon be over.

Too late, my brothers, too late,
But never mind.
All my trials, Lord, soon be over.

There is a tree in Paradise.
The pilgrims call it the "Tree of Life."
All my trials, Lord, soon be over.

If religion were a thing that money could buy,
The rich would live and the poor would die.
All my trials, Lord, soon be over.

Too late, my brothers, too late,
But never mind.
All my trials, Lord, soon be over.

On Top of Old Smokey

On top of Old Smokey
All covered with snow,
I lost my true lover
For a'courtin' too slow.

Now courtin's a pleasure
And partin's a grief,
But a false-hearted lover
Is worse than a thief.

'Cause a thief, he will rob you
And take what you have,
But a false-hearted lover
Will take you to your grave.

And the grave will decay you
And turn you to dust,
But where is the young man
That a poor girl can trust.

They'll hug you and kiss you
And tell you more lies
Than the crossties on railroads
Or the stars in the sky.

They'll tell you they love you
To give your heart ease,
But the moment your back's turned,
They'll court whom they please.

Bury me on Old Smokey,
Old Smokey so high,
So the wild birds in heaven
Will hear my sad cry.

On top of Old Smokey
All covered with snow,
I lost my true lover
For a'courtin' too slow.

Who's Gonna Shoe Your Pretty Little Foot

Who's gonna shoe your pretty little foot?
Who's gonna glove your hand?
Who's gonna kiss your red ruby lips?
And who's gonna be your man?

Who's gonna be your man, love?
Who's gonna be your man?
Who's gonna kiss your red ruby lips?
And who's gonna be your man?

Mama will shoe your pretty little foot,
Daddy will glove your hand.
Sister will kiss your red ruby lips,
And you don't need no man.

You don't need no man, love,
You don't need no man.
Sister's gonna kiss your red ruby lips,
And you don't need no man.

The longest train I ever did see
Was a hundred coaches long.
The only girl I ever did love
Was on that train and gone.

On that train and gone, love,
On that train and gone.
The only girl I ever did love
Was on that train and gone.

Brahms' Lullaby

Lullaby and good night, with dreams now in flight,
And lilies be spread over baby's wee bed.

Lay thee down now and rest, may thy slumber be blessed.
Lay thee down now and rest, may thy slumber be blessed.

Lullaby and good night, thy mother's delight,
Bright angels will fly round my dearest, abide.

They will guard thee at rest, as thou sleep on my breast.
They will guard thee at rest, as thou sleep on my breast.

Notes to My Fellow "Pickers"

As you review the lyrics to the songs printed on the following pages, you will see the chord names (with diagrams showing you where to put your fingers on the strings) above the words indicating where each new chord begins.

Please don't feel you have to stick with the chords I'm playing at all. I'm always changing and developing my accompaniments—sometimes I change back to earlier chord patterns, then return again. In folk music, making these changes is not only allowed, it's expected and admired as part of a music that celebrates the gifts of each individual to interpret the music as he or she sees fit. Making changes to a folk song is called "the folk process," which means that new players change the song's lyrics, melody, rhythmic feel, and accompaniment to suit themselves and make the song feel right and relevant in their own times.

Have fun creating your own folk process.
The songs will appreciate it and feel loved, I promise you.

All Through the Night

C   Am   D   G   F   G   C

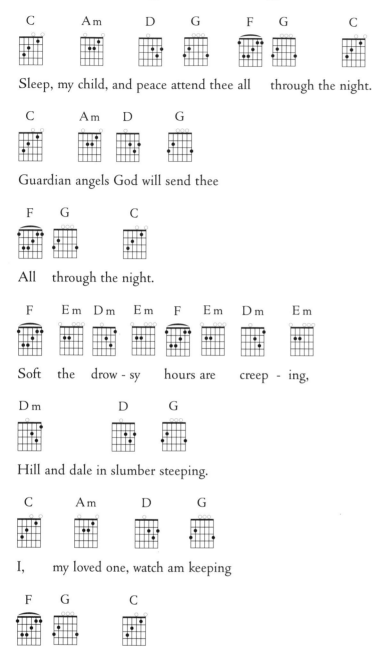

Sleep, my child, and peace attend thee all   through the night.

C   Am   D   G

Guardian angels God will send thee

F   G   C

All   through the night.

F   Em   Dm   Em   F   Em   Dm   Em

Soft   the   drow - sy   hours are   creep - ing,

Dm   D   G

Hill and dale in slumber steeping.

C   Am   D   G

I,   my loved one, watch am keeping

F   G   C

All   through the night.

32

Puff, the Magic Dragon

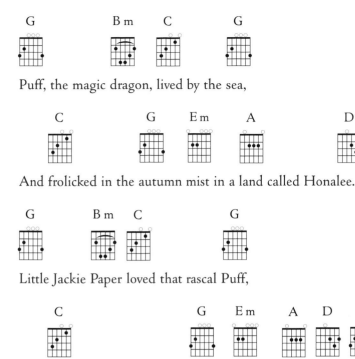

Puff, the magic dragon, lived by the sea,

And frolicked in the autumn mist in a land called Honalee.

Little Jackie Paper loved that rascal Puff,

And brought him strings and sealing wax and other fancy stuff.

Puff, the magic dragon, lived by the sea,
And frolicked in the autumn mist in a land called Honalee.
Puff, the magic dragon, lived by the sea,
And frolicked in the autumn mist in a land called Honalee.

Together they would travel on a boat with billowed sail.
Jackie kept a lookout perched on Puff's gigantic tail.
Noble kings and princes would bow whene'er they came.
Pirate ships would lower their flag when Puff roared out his name.

Puff, the magic dragon, lived by the sea,
And frolicked in the autumn mist in a land called Honalee.
Puff, the magic dragon, lived by the sea,
And frolicked in the autumn mist in a land called Honalee.

A dragon lives forever, but not so little girls and boys.
Painted wings and giants' rings make way for other toys.
One gray night it happened, Jackie Paper came no more,
So Puff, that mighty dragon, he ceased his fearless roar.

His head was bent in sorrow, and green scales fell like rain.
Puff no longer went to play along the cherry lane.
Without his lifelong friend, Puff could not be brave,
So Puff, that mighty dragon, sadly slipped into his cave.

Puff, the magic dragon, lives by the sea,
And frolics in the autumn mist in a land called Honalee.
Puff, the magic dragon, still lives by the sea,
And frolics in the autumn mist in a land called Honalee.

Ole Blue

C

I had a dog and his name was Blue,

G   C

I had a dog and his name was Blue,

C

I had a dog and his name was Blue,

G   C

I betcha five dollars he's a good dog too.

C   Am   G   C

Cryin', "Here, Blue! You good dog, you."

Ole Blue come when I blow my horn,
Ole Blue come when I blow my horn.
Blue come a-runnin' through the yellow corn.
Ole Blue come when I blow my horn.

Cryin', "Here, Blue! You good dog, you."

Blue chased a possum up a hollow limb,
Blue chased a possum up a hollow limb,
Blue chased a possum up a hollow limb,
Ole Blue growled, possum grinned at him.

Cryin', "Here, Blue! You good dog, you."

When Ole Blue died, he died so hard,
Ole Blue died, he died so hard,
Ole Blue died, he died so hard,
He shook the ground in my backyard.

Cryin', "Here, Blue! You good dog, you."

One more thing you got to know,
One more thing before you go,
One more thing you got to know,
Blue's gone to heaven where the good dogs go.

Cryin', "Here, Blue! You good dog, you."

I had a dog and his name was Blue,
I had a dog and his name was Blue,
I had a dog and his name was Blue,
I betcha five dollars he's a good dog too.

Cryin', "Here, Blue! You good dog, you."
Cryin', "Here, Blue! You good dog, you."

All the Pretty Little Horses

Am   D   Dm

Hush-a-bye, don't you cry,

C   E7   Am

Go to sleepy, little baby.

Am   D   Dm

When you wake, you shall   have

C   E7   Am

All the pretty little horses.

C   Am

Dapples and grays, pintos and bays,

Em   E7   Am

All the pretty little horses.

Way down yonder, in the meadow,
Poor little baby crying, "Mama."
Bees and the butterflies flutter round its eyes,
Poor little baby crying, "Mama."

Hush-a-bye, don't you cry,
Go to sleepy, little baby.
When you wake, you shall have
All the pretty little horses.

Hush, Little Baby

C   G

Hush, little baby, don't say a word,

C

Mama's gonna buy you a mockingbird.

C   G

And if that mockingbird don't sing,

C

Papa's gonna buy you a diamond ring.

And if that diamond ring turns brass,
Mama's gonna buy you a looking glass.

And if that looking glass gets broke,
Papa's gonna buy you a billy goat.

And if that billy goat don't pull,
Mama's gonna buy you a cart and bull.

And if that cart and bull turns over,
Papa's gonna buy you a doggie named Rover.

And if that doggie named Rover don't bark,
Mama's gonna buy you a horse and cart.

And if that horse and cart falls down,
You'll still be the sweetest little baby in town.

Kumbaya

C   F   C

Kumbaya, my Lord, kumbaya,

Em   Dm   G

Kumbaya, my Lord kumbaya,

C   F   C

Kumbaya, my Lord, kumbaya,

F   C   G   C

Oh,   Lord,   kumbaya.

Someone's singing, Lord, kumbaya,
Someone's singing, Lord, kumbaya,
Someone's singing, Lord, kumbaya,
Oh, Lord, kumbaya.

Someone's laughing, Lord, kumbaya,
Someone's laughing, Lord, kumbaya,
Someone's laughing, Lord, kumbaya,
Oh, Lord, kumbaya.

Someone's crying, Lord, kumbaya,
Someone's crying, Lord, kumbaya,
Someone's crying, Lord, kumbaya,
Oh, Lord, kumbaya.

Someone's praying, Lord, kumbaya,
Someone's praying, Lord, kumbaya,
Someone's praying, Lord, kumbaya,
Oh, Lord, kumbaya.

Someone's sleeping, Lord, kumbaya,
Someone's sleeping, Lord, kumbaya,
Someone's sleeping, Lord, kumbaya,
Oh, Lord, kumbaya.

The Water Is Wide

(If you place your capo on the second fret and play in the key of C major, this song will sound in the same key as on the CD: D major.)

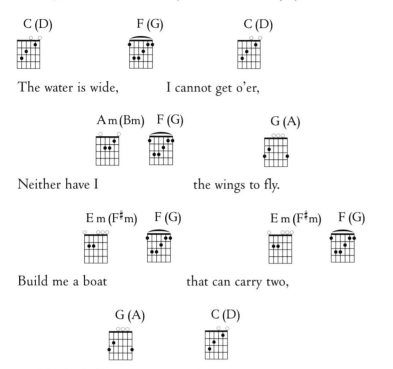

C (D)   F (G)   C (D)

The water is wide,   I cannot get o'er,

Am (Bm) F (G)   G (A)

Neither have I   the wings to fly.

Em (F♯m) F (G)   Em (F♯m) F (G)

Build me a boat   that can carry two,

G (A)   C (D)

And both shall row, my love and I.

I leaned my back against an oak,
Thinking it was a trusty tree.
But first it bent and then it broke,
Just as my love proved false to me.

Oh, love is handsome and love is fine,
Gay as a jewel when first it's new.
But love grows old and it waxeth cold,
And fades away like morning dew.

The water is wide, I cannot get o'er,
Neither have I the wings to fly.
Build me a boat that can carry two,
And both shall row, my love and I.

Down in the Valley

C   G

Down in the valley, the valley so low,

C

Hang your head over, hear the wind blow.

G

Hear the wind blow, love, hear the wind blow,

C

Hang your head over, hear the wind blow.

Roses love sunshine, violets love dew,
Angels in heaven knows I love you.
Knows I love you, dear, knows I love you,
Angels in heaven knows I love you.

I knew I loved you, right from the start.
Say that you love me, and we'll never part.
We'll never part, love, we'll never part.
Say that you love me, we'll never part.

Down in the valley, the valley so low,
Hang your head over, hear the wind blow.
Hear the wind blow, love, hear the wind blow,
Hang your head over, hear the wind blow.

All My Trials

C   G m

Hush, little baby, don't you cry,

C   E m   F

You know your mama   someday will fly.

C   A m   D m   G   C

All   my trials, Lord, soon be over.

I had a little book was given to me,
And every page spelled liberty.
All my trials, Lord, soon be over.

C   G m

Too late, my brothers,   too late,

F

But never mind.

C   A m   D m   G   C

All   my trials, Lord, soon be over.

There is a tree in Paradise.
The pilgrims call it the "Tree of Life."
All my trials, Lord, soon be over.

If religion were a thing that money could buy,
The rich would live and the poor would die.
All my trials, Lord, soon be over.

Too late, my brothers, too late,
But never mind.
All my trials, Lord, soon be over.

On Top of Old Smokey

(If you place your capo on the second fret and play in the key of G major, this song will sound in the same key as on the CD: A major.)

G (A)   C (D)

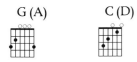

On top of Old Smokey

G (A)

All covered with snow,

D (E)

I lost my true lover

D 7 (E 7)   G (A)

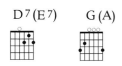

For a'courtin' too slow.

Now courtin's a pleasure
And partin's a grief,
But a false-hearted lover
Is worse than a thief.

'Cause a thief, he will rob you
And take what you have,
But a false-hearted lover
Will take you to your grave.

And the grave will decay you
And turn you to dust,
But where is the young man
That a poor girl can trust.

They'll hug you and kiss you
And tell you more lies
Than the crossties on railroads
Or the stars in the sky.

They'll tell you they love you
To give your heart ease,
But the moment your back's turned,
They'll court whom they please.

Bury me on Old Smokey,
Old Smokey so high,
So the wild birds in heaven
Will hear my sad cry.

On top of Old Smokey
All covered with snow,
I lost my true lover
For a'courtin' too slow.

Who's Gonna Shoe Your Pretty Little Foot

(If you place your capo on the second fret and play in the key of G major, this song will sound in the same key as on the CD: A major.)

G (A)   G⁷ (A⁷)

Who's gonna shoe your pretty little foot?

C (D)   G (A)

Who's gonna glove your hand?

C (D)   G (A)   E m (F♯m)

Who's gonna kiss your red ruby lips?

A m (Bm)   D (E)   G (A)

And who's gonna be your man?

E m (F♯m)   B m (C♯m)

Who's gonna be your man, love?

C (D)   G (A)

Who's gonna be your man?

A m (Bm)   D (E)   G (A)   E m (F♯m)

Who's gonna kiss your red ruby lips?

A m (Bm)   D (E)   G (A)

And who's gonna be your man?

Mama will shoe your pretty little foot,
Daddy will glove your hand.
Sister will kiss your red ruby lips,
And you don't need no man.

You don't need no man, love,
You don't need no man.
Sister's gonna kiss your red ruby lips,
And you don't need no man.

The longest train I ever did see
Was a hundred coaches long.
The only girl I ever did love
Was on that train and gone.

On that train and gone, love,
On that train and gone.
The only girl I ever did love
Was on that train and gone.

Brahms' Lullaby

G   D

Lullaby and good night, with dreams now in flight,

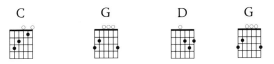

G

And lilies be spread over baby's wee bed.

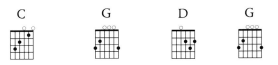

C   G   D   G

Lay thee down now and rest, may thy slumber be blessed.

C   G   D   G

Lay thee down now and rest, may thy slumber be blessed.

Lullaby and good night, thy mother's delight,
Bright angels will fly round my dearest, abide.

They will guard thee at rest, as thou sleep on my breast.
They will guard thee at rest, as thou sleep on my breast.

About the Songs

All Through the Night

This song was a great favorite of mine to sing for my children, Bethany and Christopher. If they had a bad dream or were afraid of the dark, this lullaby, translated from the eighteenth-century Welsh folk song "Ar Hyd y Nos," would reassure them that I would always be there to watch over them and make sure they were safe.

Puff, the Magic Dragon

I cowrote this song with my good friend Lenny Lipton while we were in college at Cornell University. For most people, this song has become something more than a touching tale about a little boy and a dragon who love each other. "Puff" has come to symbolize many of the dynamic changes that took place in America in the 1960s, epitomizing a new spirit of kindness and the search for peace both on a personal and worldwide scale.

Ole Blue

One of the most beloved, endearing story songs I've ever sung for children, "Ole Blue" tells of the great love between a child and a dog. We can sense how proud the child is that Blue responds whenever he hears the sound of the child's horn, and the child's delightful appreciation of Blue's way of chasing a possum up a tree. Particularly touching is the child's confirmation that Blue is a really "good dog" and has, like all dogs, a place in heaven.

All the Pretty Little Horses

This is a song about a slave mother's longing for fairness and justice for her child. In the days of slavery, African-American mothers, who cared for the babies of their masters, frequently had to leave their own children in shacks and fields with no one to watch over them. The sympathetic way this song tells how mothers yearned to be with and take care of their own babies was part of the way songs helped to change attitudes toward slavery and other painful forms of injustice.

Hush, Little Baby

One of the most famous American lullabies, this song is comforting because it answers the most lighthearted childhood wishes while promising that no matter what misfortune a child encounters, mommy and daddy will make everything turn out all right. The poetic twist in the last line assures us that even if events disappoint, the child will continue to be loved, which is the most important thing of all.

Kumbaya

In "Kumbaya," a song that originated in Africa, the singer humbly asks the Lord to "come by here" and be present throughout the ups and downs of life. This request, when shared in this gentle song, creates a strong feeling of togetherness among those who are singing. This sense of community is one of the great gifts folk songs bring us when we sing them.

The Water Is Wide

"The Water Is Wide" is many people's favorite folk song, and one of mine as well. It is ironic how, in this lament, the spirit of the song seems to glorify love, despite its painful disappointments. The symbolism of the boat crossing o'er the water, as well as the "wings to fly," describe the pain endured when one is unable to revive love. Ultimately, we are left more enthralled by love than before we heard the song. Such is the poetry of folk music.

Down in the Valley

In this classic lullaby, love for baby becomes combined with remembered longing, wistful memory, and hopeful promise, all conveyed as a blessing for the child or baby to whom you are singing. I used to imagine that I was rocking Bethany or Christopher in a swing when I would sing this song to them at bedtime. My heart would say to them, "Life is a blessing, with all its ups and downs. Live life fully, live it with gratitude and optimism, and even cherish the moments that are less than wonderful. They, too, can be blessings in their own way."

All My Trials

To me, this Bahamian lullaby is perhaps the most touching, and in some ways the most inspiring, of the songs on this CD. When I sing it, I feel the amazing strength of the mother, a slave who comforts her baby even as she acknowledges that her own life will soon be over. The mother is at peace with the world as she sings about faith and liberty, which she asserts are the core of life. The mother's selflessness inspires us and reveals, above all, her love for her child who is, to her, the most important thing in the world.

On Top of Old Smokey

This song is a heartbreaking expression of what I believe to be a universal yearning for a love that will last a lifetime. There is great anger and pain expressed in this song, even bitterness, over betrayal and love lost. But in the end, the musical beauty of this classic lament conveys the feeling that, if given the choice, the person singing it would not trade his or her memories of love for anything. We come to see this pain as a measure of the depth of the beautiful love once shared.

Who's Gonna Shoe Your Pretty Little Foot

At one time, looking at life ahead, all a girl would need was a man to shoe her foot (give her a home), glove her hand (provide her with clothes and social acceptability), and kiss her red ruby lips (love her) and she would, presumably, be set for life. In this lullaby, the baby girl is assured that, at least for a while, mommy, daddy, and sister will provide for all her needs. In today's world, most girls are no longer dependent upon men when they grow up, so in this sense this song is really outmoded—though now, as ever, romantic love remains a gamble at best.

Brahms' Lullaby

Johannes Brahms, one of the greatest classical music composers of the nineteenth century, wrote amazing symphonies and very complex pieces for a wide range of instruments. But he also wrote this beautiful, elegant, and simple song that uses only three chords. At first, I tried to change some of the chords to personalize it, but in the end I left it as it was written, finding the wisdom of Brahms, like the wisdom of folk songs, essential to respect and hard to improve upon.

About the Author

Peter Yarrow's career has spanned close to five decades as a member of the legendary folk trio Peter, Paul, & Mary, who became known to many as a voice of their generation's conscience, awakening and inspiring others to help make the world a more just, equitable, and peaceful place. Today, Yarrow devotes the majority of his time to running Operation Respect, a nonprofit he founded in 1999 that received a unanimous vote of Congress honoring its work to create respectful, safe, and bully-free environments for children in schools across America and beyond. Besides numerous awards for his artistry and his public service, Peter has received two honorary doctorates for his steadfast work in the educational arena.

For many years, Peter Yarrow dreamed of recording his favorite folk songs in a very simple, intimate way—the way he first heard them sung as a child. Along with his daughter, Bethany Yarrow, a gifted singer in her own right, Peter shares the songs that first moved and inspired him to become the renowned folk singer he is today. When asked what he would most want to give the generations that follow him, Peter said, "I would give them these songs that helped me come to realize what, for me, is really important in life—people, love, work, and service to each other. I believe that all children can be helped to discover what's important to them in their lives, through these songs. It's magic, in a way, but it seems to happen every time!"

About the Illustrator

Terry Widener's relationship with folk music began as a child in Oklahoma, where he was surrounded by classic folk songs performed by singers like Woody Guthrie. Folk music had made a big impact on the region during the Dustbowl era, and as Terry grew up, this music was an essential part of his heritage.

Inspired by a passion for art, Terry studied graphic design at the University of Tulsa. He has illustrated more than twenty books, including *If the Shoe Fits* by Gary Soto, *Steel Town* by Jonah Winter, and *Lou Gehrig: The Luckiest Man* by David Adler. His picture books have won numerous accolades including a Boston Globe–Horn Book Honor Award, an ALA Notable Children's Book Award, and the California Young Reader Medal.

A father of three, Terry currently resides in McKinney, Texas, with his wife, Leslie.

CD Credits

CD Produced by Peter Yarrow

Peter Yarrow: Lead Vocals, Guitar

Bethany Yarrow: Lead Vocals

Mary Rower: Background Vocals on "On Top of Old Smokey" and "Down in the Valley"

Paul Prestopino: Banjo, Mandolin, Mandola, Guitars (6 string and 12 string), Dobro, Ukulele, Harmonica

Recorded at Midwood Studios, Brooklyn, New York

Recording Engineer: Glen Marshall

First Mix Engineers: Glen Marshall, Tom Swift

Final Mix Engineer: Kevin Salem, Woodstock, New York

Mastering Conversion & Mastering Prep: Kevin Salem, Woodstock, New York

Mastering: Howie Weinberg, Masterdisk, New York, New York

PY Productions Staff: Beth Bradford, Rachel Jackson, Tony Arancio

Musical transcriptions by Robert Agis

Special Thanks

Paula Allen, Tony Arancio, Beth Bradford, Che and Zachary Cappadocia, Louise Daniels, Kaylee Davis, Meaghan Finnerty, Frances Gilbert, Sebastian Gross-Ossa, Rachel Jackson, Marcus Leaver, Bill Luckey, Charlie Nurnberg, Valentina Ossa, Lisa Palattella, Scott Piehl, Mary Rower, Jacquie Turner, Mary Beth Yarrow.